Eco-Mania Mazes

Jessica Mazurkiewicz

Dover Publications, Inc.
Mineola, New York

Bibliographical Note

Eco-Mania Mazes is a new work, first published by Dover Publications, Inc., in 2010.

International Standard Book Number

ISBN-13: 978-0-486-47561-5
ISBN-10: 0-486-47561-1

Manufactured in the United States by Courier Corporation
47561101
www.doverpublications.com

Note

Everybody is "going green" lately. This means that we are trying to find ways to help our environment by using less energy, reducing our trash, and reusing products. The mazes and captions in this book will give you some ideas on how you can become eco-friendly. Hanging clothes out to dry instead of using a dryer, eating fresh fruit instead of individually packaged snacks, and using both sides of a piece of paper are just some of the suggestions you will find in this fun and informative activity book. If you need help with a maze, or if you want to check your answers, the solutions begin on page 52.

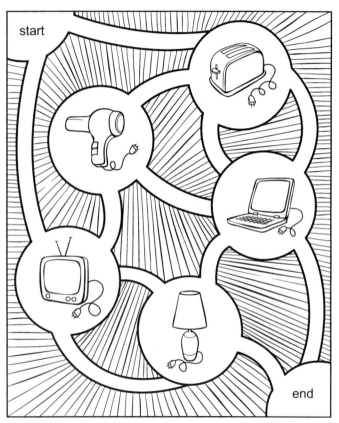

Using less electricity helps to put fewer greenhouse gases into the air. Make sure electricity is saved by finding a path through the maze that goes by each electric object.

start

end

Clean the creek for the beavers by guiding the
garbage through the maze to the recycle bins.

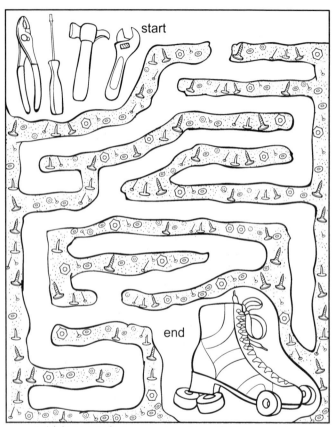

start

end

Add less trash to your local landfill by repairing
broken toys and items instead of throwing them away.
Bring the tools through the maze to repair
the broken rollerskates.

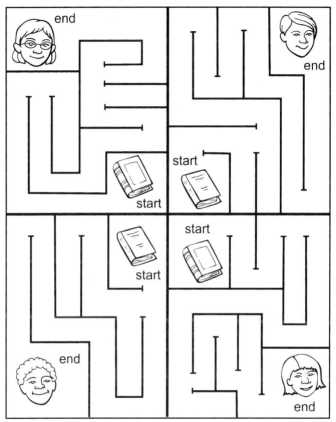

You can save paper by swapping books, magazines,
and comics with friends instead of buying new ones.
Help the children swap books by guiding a
book through the maze to each of them.

7

A great way to help the planet is by volunteering at a nature preserve. Help the volunteer by guiding her through the forest maze.

8

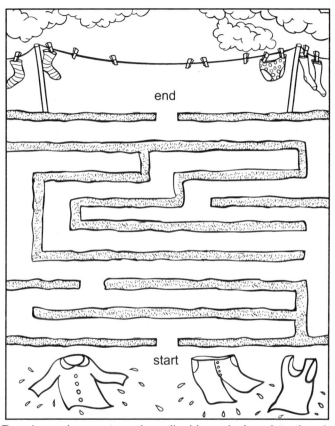

end

start

Running a dryer puts carbon dioxide emissions into the air. You can help the environment by hanging your laundry outside whenever possible. Can you bring the wet clothes through the grass maze to the clothesline at the end?

start

end

Bug sprays can pollute the air. Instead of using
chemicals and sprays, leave alone any spiders you
find in your home or yard so they can catch pest bugs.
Can you guide the spider through the maze to her web?
10

start

end

Many animals are losing their natural habitats. You can
help by creating a wildlife garden to attract local
birds and insects. Can you guide the
hummingbird through the garden maze?

11

end

start

Because of rising temperatures the polar ice caps are
melting. Can you guide the polar bear from one
iceberg to another through the water maze?

start

end

Help to replace the tree that was cut down by guiding
the sapling through the maze to where it will be planted.

13

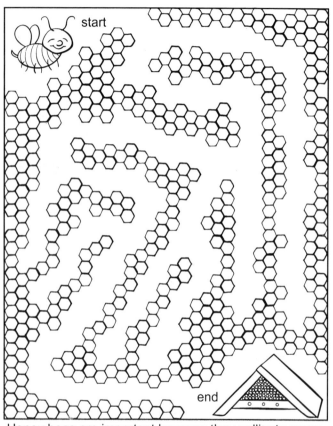

start

end

Honey bees are important because they pollinate many
of the foods that we eat. You can help honey bees by
creating a bee shelter where solitary bees can rest.
Can you lead the bee through the maze to the shelter?
14

start

end

You can help the environment by eating snacks like fruits and vegetables instead of individually packaged snacks like candy or chips. Can you find a path through the maze that brings the unpackaged snacks to each child?

15

start

end

Air fresheners pollute the air. You can use houseplants
instead as a natural air freshener. Can you bring the
air through the maze so it can be purified by the plant?

16

Visit your local library to learn more about global warming
and changes that you can make to help the environment.
Help the girl learn what steps she can take by
guiding her through the library maze.

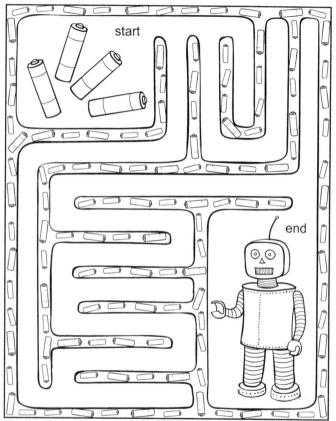

start

end

Disposable batteries release dangerous chemicals into
the environment. Instead, try rechargeable batteries
that can be used many times. Bring rechargeable
batteries through the maze to power the toy robot.

18

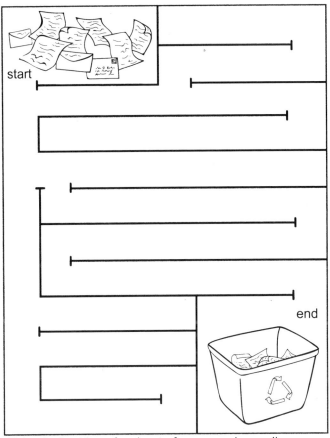

start

end

Using both sides of a sheet of paper and recycling your used paper helps to save trees. Can you guide the used paper through the maze to the recycle bin?

19

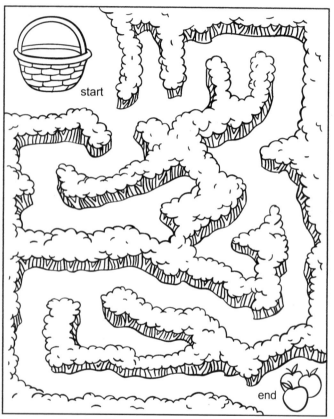

start

end

Transporting food long distances is a major contributor
to global warming. You can help by purchasing local
produce or shopping at farmer's markets.
Find your way through the orchard maze to the apples.

20

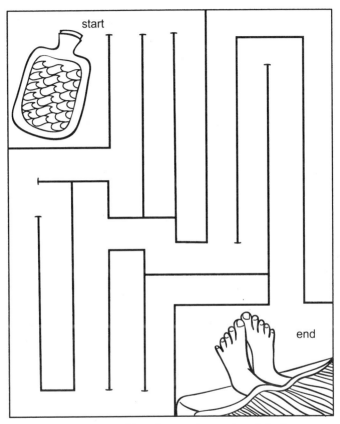

Electric blankets and heating pads waste a lot of energy.
You can help the environment by using a hot water
bottle instead. Can you bring the hot water
bottle through the maze to warm the cold feet?

start

end

Balloons that are released into the air can cause power
outages and injure sea turtles and whales. Bring the
balloons through the city maze to the house at the end.

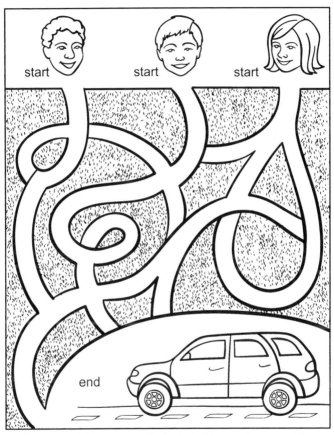

A group of friends wants to help the environment by carpooling. Can you lead each of them through the maze to the car at the end?

You can help to conserve our natural resources by
sharing or trading toys with friends instead of buying new.
Help the friends exchange toys by guiding a toy
through the maze to each child.

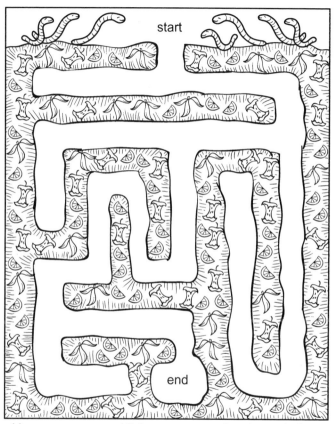

start

end

You can save your kitchen scraps and make an indoor wormery where worms will break the scraps down into a compost that you can use for plants. Help the worms create compost by bringing them through the scrap maze.

25

end

start

You can help your local wildlife by keeping your cat
inside at night where it can't harm other animals.
Guide the cat through the backyard maze
to bring her in for the night.

26

start

end

Instead of using an air conditioner, try using a fan to cool off. They are great for the environment because they use a lot less energy. Cool off the children by leading the breeze from the fan through the maze.

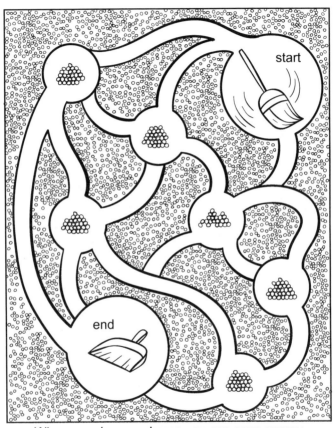

start

end

When you do your chores you can save energy
by using a broom and dustpan when possible instead
of using a vacuum. Can you find a path through the
maze that brings the broom by each pile of dust?

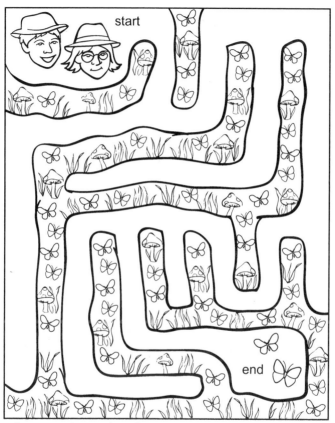

start

end

As you enjoy and explore nature make sure to stick to
footpaths so you won't flatten important wildlife.
Can you help the hikers enjoy nature by guiding
them through to the end of the trail?

29

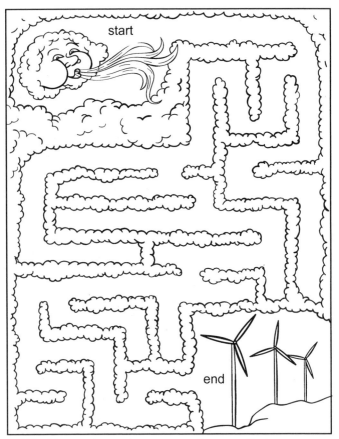

start

end

Wind is an alternative source of energy that causes
no damage to the environment. Guide the wind
through the cloud maze to the turbines.

30

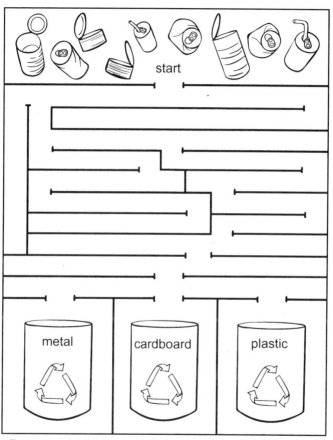

start

metal

cardboard

plastic

Recycling helps to conserve our natural resources and save energy. Can you guide the tin cans through the maze to the proper recycling bin?

31

start

end

Using biodegradable pencils and refillable pens instead of disposables for your schoolwork helps to conserve our natural resources. Can you bring the eco-friendly pens and pencils through the maze to the children?

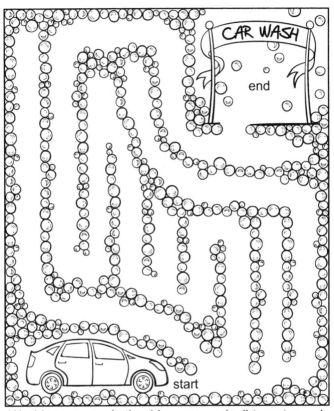

Washing your car in the driveway sends dirty water and
chemicals into the stormdrains, streams, rivers, and
lakes. Instead take your vehicle to the carwash,
where the run-off chemicals are disposed of safely.
Bring the car through the maze to the carwash.

start

end

Woodpeckers are an endangered species that have lost
much of their natural habitat. Help the woodpecker
find a safe home by guiding it through the maze.

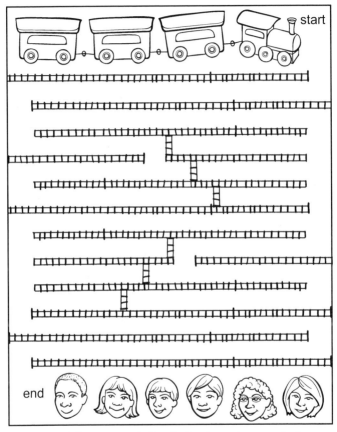

Using public transportation helps to reduce emissions
into the air. Guide the train through the
track maze to the waiting passengers.

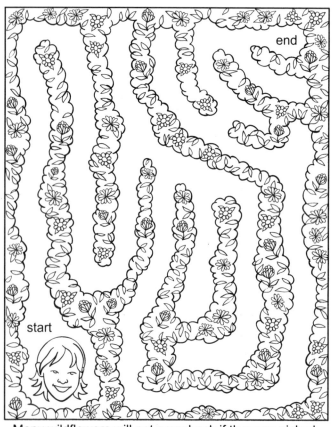

start

end

Many wildflowers will not grow back if they are picked.
Make sure that there is nature for everyone to enjoy
by leaving wildflowers where you find them.
Can you guide the girl through the wildflower maze?

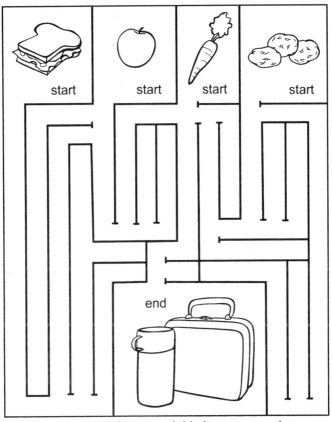

start   start   start   start

end

Bringing your lunch in a recyclable brown paper bag or a
reusable metal container helps to keep a lot of plastic
out of our landfills. Can you fill the lunchbox by
guiding each piece of food through the maze?

37

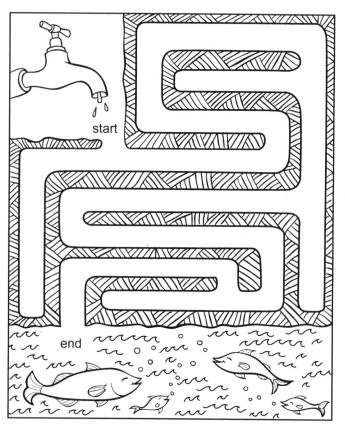

start

end

Help to conserve water by taking baths or quick showers
and turning the water off when brushing your teeth.
Guide the conserved water through the pipe maze
to the lake where it can be enjoyed by everyone.

You can reduce the number of trees that are cut down by requesting not to receive junk mail. Guide the junk mail through the maze to return it to the sender.

If you are chilly you can help the environment by
adding layers instead of turning up the heat.
Can you bring each warm item through the maze?

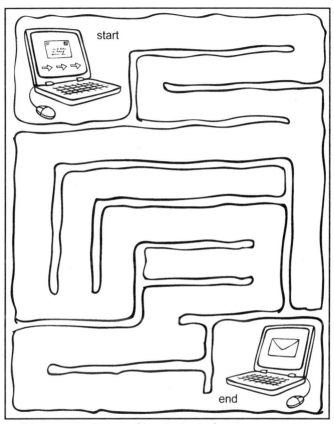

When you write to a friend who is far away you can
help the environment by sending an email instead.
Can you bring the electronic mail through the
maze from one computer to the other?

41

start

end

You can conserve electricity by spending less time
playing video games and watching television and more
time playing outdoors. Bring the boy through
the park maze to join his friends.

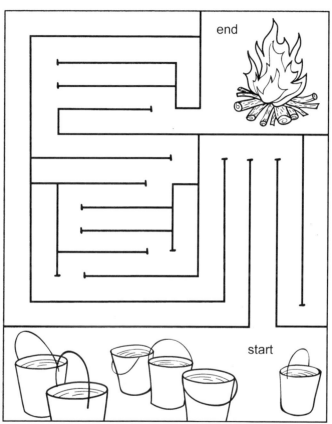

Forest fires cause massive damage to plants and
animals. Always practice fire safety and make sure
to put out campfires fully. Guide the buckets
of water through the maze to put the fire out.

43

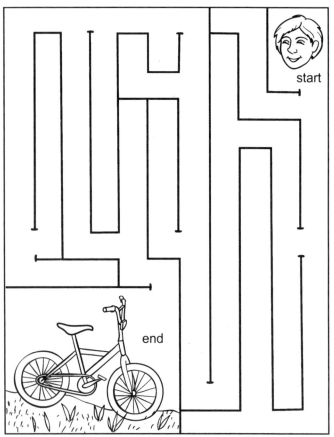

start

end

You can help make the air cleaner by walking or biking
instead of driving whenever possible. Help the boy
find his bicycle by leading him through the maze.

44

You can help the environment by donating old clothes or making them into something new like a blanket, pillow, or stuffed toy. Can you bring the old clothes through the maze to the sewing station?

end

start

Many dolphins are harmed every year when they become entangled in fishing nets. Help the dolphins by guiding them through the net maze and by eating dolphin-safe tuna.

start

end

Solar energy is a way of generating electricity that is great
for the environment and uses energy from the sun.
Can you guide the suns rays through the
maze to the solar panels below?

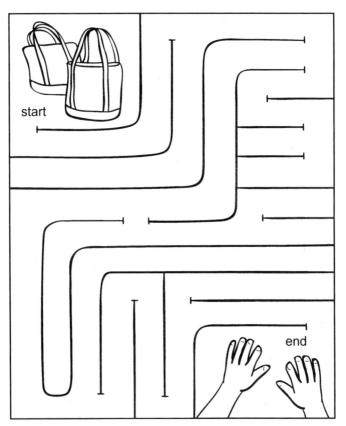

Plastic bags are very damaging to the environment because they aren't biodegradable. You can help by using paper bags or reusable fabric bags.
Can you guide the fabric totebag through the maze?

You can help the environment by telling people
what steps you are taking to help the planet.
Can you find a path through the maze that
will spread the word to each person?

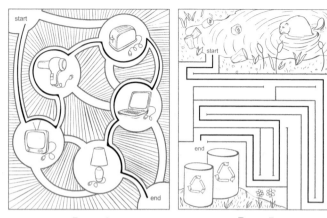

Page 4

Page 5

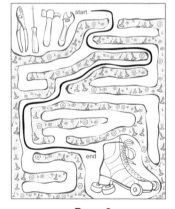

Page 6

Page 7

52

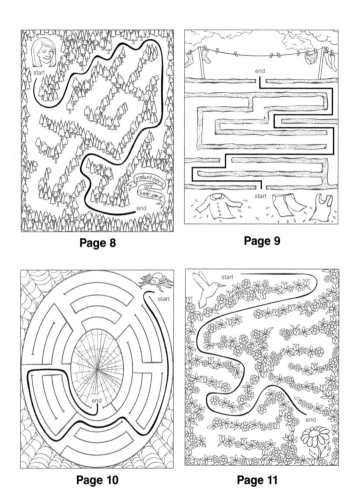

Page 8

Page 9

Page 10

Page 11

53

Page 12

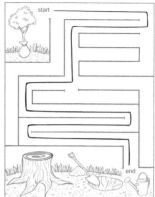

Page 13

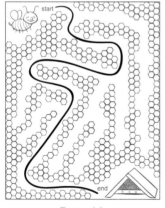

Page 14

Page 15

Page 16

Page 17

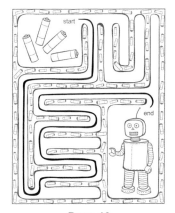

Page 18

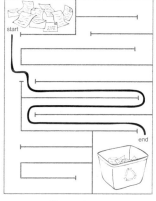

Page 19

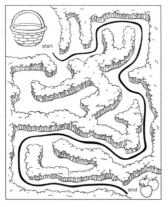

Page 20

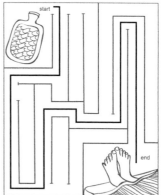

Page 21

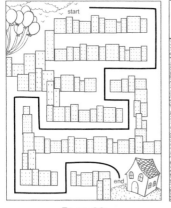

Page 22

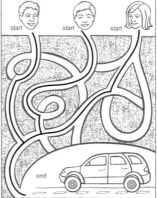

Page 23

Page 24

Page 25

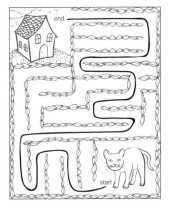

Page 26

Page 27

57

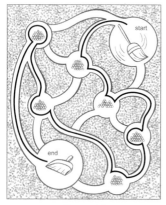

Page 28

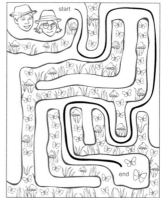

Page 29

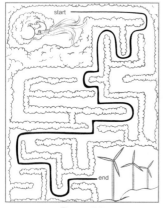

Page 30

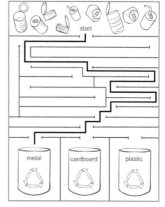

Page 31

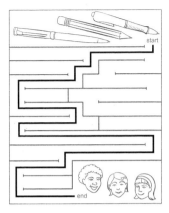

Page 32

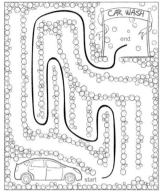

Page 33

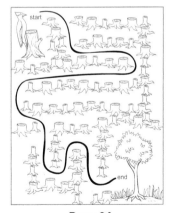

Page 34

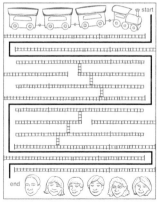

Page 35

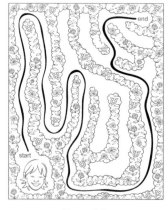

Page 36

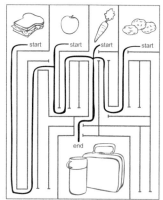

Page 37

Page 38

Page 39

Page 40

Page 41

Page 42

Page 43

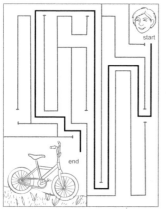

Page 44

Page 45

Page 46

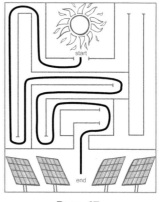

Page 47

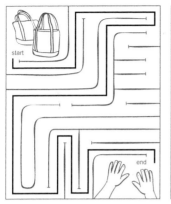

Page 48

Page 49